OP Notable Illustrator

For Chloe

Duck
Text copyright © 1988 by David Lloyd
Illustrations copyright © 1988 by Charlotte Voake
Printed in Italy. For information address Junior Books,
10 East 53rd Street, J. B. Lippincott New York, N.Y. 10022.
Printed in Italy. All rights reserved.
1 2 3 4 5 6 7 8 9 10
First American Edition

Library of Congress Cataloging-in-Publication Data
Lloyd, David, 1945–
   Duck.

   Summary: A little boy calls all animals "duck"
and all vehicles "truck" until his grandmother
gives him a little help.
   [1. Grandmothers—Fiction.   2. Animals—Fiction.
3. Vehicles—Fiction]   I. Voake, Charlotte, ill.
II. Title.
PZ7.L774Du 1988   [E]   87-26200
ISBN 0-397-32274-7
ISBN 0-397-32275-5

Duck

Written by David Lloyd
Illustrated by Charlotte Voake

J. B. Lippincott   New York

There was a time,
long ago,
when Tim called
all animals duck.

"Duck," Tim said.

"Horse," said Granny.

"Duck," Tim said.

"Sheep," said Granny.

"Duck," Tim said.

"Chicken,"
said Granny.

So Granny took
Tim to the pond.
"Duck," she said.

Tim looked and
looked.
"Duck," he said.
Granny kissed him.

A little later
Tim saw a tractor.

"Truck," he said.

A little later
Tim saw a bus.

"Truck," he said.

A little later
Tim saw an old car.

"Truck," he said.

So Granny showed
Tim a truck.
"Truck," she said.

Tim looked and
looked.
"Truck," he said.
Granny kissed him.

For some time after
this Tim never said a
single word.
He just looked and
looked.

He looked at his
train. He looked at
his truck.
But he never said a
single word.

Then Granny took
Tim to the pond
again.
Tim saw the duck.
He looked and
looked.

The duck said, "Quack!"

"Duck," Tim said.
"Duck," Granny said.
Granny kissed Tim.
Tim kissed Granny.